New Kid in Town

Janette Oke's Animal Friends

Spunky's Diary
The Prodigal Cat
The Impatient Turtle
This Little Pig
New Kid in Town
Ducktails

JANETTE OKE'S

Animal Friends

New Kid in Town

Illustrated by Nancy Munger

New Kid in Town
Revised, full-color edition 2001
Copyright © 1983, 2001
Janette Oke

Illustrations by Nancy Munger
Design by Jennifer Parker

Published by Bethany House Publishers
A Ministry of Bethany Fellowship International
11400 Hampshire Avenue South
Minneapolis, Minnesota 55438
www.bethanyhouse.com

Printed in China

Library of Congress Catalog Number 00011554

ISBN 0–7642–2449-2

Dedicated to Mary Frank teacher
and my "special" life-long friend,
Eleanor Quantz.

JANETTE OKE was born in Champion, Alberta, during the depression years, to a Canadian prairie farmer and his wife. She is a graduate of Mountain View Bible College in Didsbury, Alberta, where she met her husband, Edward. Both Janette and Edward have been active in their local church as Sunday school teachers and board members. The Okes have four grown children and several grandchildren and make their home near Calgary, Alberta.

CHAPTER
One

"Fuzzle!"

Mother's sharp voice brought my attention back to what I was supposed to be doing. Mother wanted us to obey the rules, and falling behind the rest of the family was high on her list of bad behavior. I jerked back my curious nose and trotted on down the trail.

This was our training period. We were the students—all six of us—and Mother was the teacher. Already we had learned how to sniff carefully before leaving the den, to walk in a line, and to listen to Mother at all times.

Mother decided when it was time to

leave the den for dinner, what was proper food for us to dine upon, and where to find water. She also decided when it was time for us to return to our beds, and once we were on the way home, she did not like dallying. I was dallying. But with Sparkey, Odar, Pokey, Phew, and little Schatze all between Mother and me, it was very easy for my attention to wander and to for-get that I was sup-posed to be marching along.

I tried. I really did. But there were so many interesting things for me to see and smell that it was very hard for me to pass them all by. So I trotted along at the end of the line, looking around and checking things out. Little by little, Mother and the rest of the family were moving farther away.

I hurried my footsteps some in an effort to catch up and tried to keep my mind on following my family. It would have worked, too, if I hadn't spotted some strange-looking boxes at the edge of Mr. Willoughby's grocery store. There was a yummy smell coming from them. I decided to get a closer look, and that's when my troubles really began.

CHAPTER
TWO

I t was a new and strange odor that greet-
ed me, but it smelled so good it made my
tummy tickle. Whatever it was, it was locked
away in the crates.

I crawled up on one of them and
pushed my nose under the lid, forcing my
head in so that I could get a better look. As I
pushed hard against the lid, I lost my foot-
ing and fell, *plop*, down upon the hard slats
of the crate bottom.

At first I was happy. I was near the
good smell, and I licked up every piece of
the goodies. I didn't know just what it was
that I was eating, but it was very tasty. I
licked the crate clean, making sure I got

every bite. When I was convinced that it truly was all gone, I decided to hurry on after Mother and the family.

Perhaps if I run fast she won't know that I was missing, I thought to myself.

As I nosed my way around the crate looking for a door, I found that it had none—at least not where I could reach it. The only opening that I could see at all was way above my head. As I looked up, I could see the opening where I had pushed my way through. Beyond that small crack the stars were starting to twinkle.

I knew that the evening would soon be giving way to night. Mother always liked to have us safely tucked away in our den by now. She would be looking for me, angry that I had fallen out of line.

As time ticked slowly by, I forgot to be scared about Mother's anger. Instead, I

became afraid that she wouldn't be able to find me. I pushed myself as near to the opening above my head as I could and even tried to jump the impossible distance a few times. It didn't work. There was no way that I could jump high enough. Still, I didn't want to give up. I jumped and clawed at the side of the box until I was exhausted.

Finally, tired and discouraged, I gave up and curled up in a corner. I would just have to wait for Mother. The crate dug into my full sides. But in spite of my discomfort, I did manage to go to sleep, hoping that it would not be too long before Mother would come back looking for me.

CHAPTER
Three

I was awakened by a lot of noise. All around me were loud, bustling people who did not seem to notice me. They were banging and clanging their way through the crates.

For a moment I was scared. What would happen when they reached mine? And then a small hope took hold of me. Why, they'd set me free, of course. Then I would be able to hurry home to Mother.

I waited excitedly for them to reach my crate. But when they did, I was not even noticed. My crate was lifted and stacked with the rest.

Then I began to move, slowly at first,

and then faster and faster, the wind whizzing and whining through the cracks of the crates.

Finally, the roaring stopped, and the humans began to lift the crates again. One after the other the crates were slammed and banged on the ground. At last they came to mine, and again I hoped that they might notice me. They didn't. They stacked my crate with the others, slammed doors, started the roaring sound again, and were gone.

After the noise had all gone away, I pressed myself to the side of the crate and looked out at the world. To my amazement, I discovered that I wasn't back where I had started from at all. In fact, I had never in my life seen the place in which the crates were now stacked.

How I wished that I had listened to Mother. She had tried so many times to warn me that my curiosity could get me into a lot of trouble. I had now learned my lesson, but would I ever find my way out?

I tried to curl up more tightly so that my empty stomach wouldn't hurt as much, but it didn't seem to help.

Finally, I just gave up and let big tears run down my furry cheeks, falling, *splash*, on the bottom of the box. Whatever would happen to me now?

CHAPTER
Four

I slept off and on, even though my own hunger told me clearly that this was not "sleeping time" but "eating time." But there was nothing to eat, and in order to forget the agony of my empty stomach, I tried hard to sleep.

Sometime during the day my napping was interrupted by a strange sound. Someone was sniffing around the crates. At first I had thought that it might be Mother, but then I remembered I was on my own now. The sniffing still continued. *Sniff, sniff, sniff.* And it was getting closer and closer.

There was bumping and shoving of the crates as the animal made his way back and forth. Finally, he came to my crate, and his sniffing made him wildly excited. He made a funny *woofing* sound and began to scratch at the lid. Even though I was sore from being in the crate all this time, I was on my feet fast!

His sniffing grew louder, and he began to push and shove even harder. The next thing I knew, my crate was tumbling and banging end-over-end. And I was tumbling and banging end-over-end, too. I wondered if I'd ever stop rolling—but at last I did.

I picked myself up and shook myself, testing to see if I had any broken bones. Everything seemed to still be in place, so I carefully took a step forward.

To my surprise and joy, I noticed that the lid had been broken off the top. There was room for me to get out. I pushed my body through the small opening, and then went to meet my helper, who was still busily sniffing at the other side of the box.

I wanted to thank him for helping me out of the crate. I guess I expected him to greet me just as eagerly as I intended to greet him—but he didn't. In fact, he took one good look at me, and his ears lifted straight up and he backed up a pace. I still trotted, rather wobbly, toward him, anxious to show my thanks. But he didn't even wait to hear them. With one wild *yip*, he turned and was gone, his tail tucked between his legs.

I don't know why he acted like he did. You would have thought that I meant him harm or something. I wondered as I watched him race away if he had ever *met* a skunk before.

CHAPTER
Five

The first order of business after being freed from the crate was to find something to eat. With my tummy growling and complaining, I decided that anything that I could chew would do. The problem seemed to be finding that something.

I set out, stiff and shaky. I sniffed the light breeze in the direction that I was headed, but no smell of food was in the air. I turned myself around, sniffing as I turned, but still no smell of food. I didn't know which direction I should go, so I just started out. Ahead I could see green things growing, tall trees and bushy shrubs. I hoped it was a place with friendly animals and food for a growing skunk.

When I reached
the edge of the forest,
I jumped into the
bushes, hoping that
my noisy approach
might scare up—not

scare off—something for my dinner. I was
disappointed. There was nothing. I slowed
to a walk, sniffing to each side of me as I
went on.

I smelled many things that were strange
to me. Other animals lived nearby—I could
tell by the scents. I wished that I could find
one of them so that I could ask him where
the food supply was. As alive and fresh as
the scents were, I never did come upon
them.

I walked on, deeper and deeper into the
woods. I was about to give up when I came

upon a wild strawberry patch. It had been well picked by other animals. But there were still a few berries here and there, and I rushed around to get them. It wasn't much, but it was better than nothing at all.

I looked up at the sky. The sun was on its way down. I needed to find a place where I could sleep. Oh, what I would have given for a tucked-away, cozy den. I had no idea where to look to find such a place. I wondered if someone would be willing to share his with me—just until I was able to find my own, of course. But there was no one around to ask.

Why, I had always thought that the forest was the friendliest place one could ever be. Now it seemed that I was totally alone. Not another creature seemed to be stirring, either in the grasses or the branches. I couldn't decide what was worse—the hunger

that gnawed at my stomach or the loneli-
ness that gnawed at my heart.

CHAPTER
Six

I looked for a long time for a place to rest. I was about to give up when I found a rotten log. I crawled in, happy that it was empty and I could make it my home.

Now, a den should be lined with soft grass and moss, only there was no time now to be out searching for that. I just curled up at the back of the log and went to sleep.

I woke the next morning to a happy surprise. Two rabbits were playing a game of tag not far from my log. I hurried forward, hoping to meet them and join in their game. But at a sharp thump from their mother's hind feet, their heads snapped up and they quickly darted for cover.

I was very sad. I had so wanted to talk
to them. Why had they hurried off? It was
almost as though they were trying to avoid
me. I hadn't done anything to upset them,
had I? I thought hard, trying to figure out
what went wrong. But after a while, I gave
up. Besides, I needed to find something to
eat and drink.

I started off, my nose working as I
went. I hadn't gone far when I thought that
I smelled water. I kept on going. Yes, very
definitely, it was water. I hurried on and
came to a small creek. It was a welcome

sight. By stretching, being careful not to lean too far, I was just able to reach my tongue to the water. What a great find! And so close to my den, as well.

Now I must get some food, I told myself and began to move away. A big splash sounded almost at my very feet. Another followed a short distance away. I stood still, listening. Out of the silence came a *croak*. It was soon joined by another, and another, and another. From all sides of me the chorus seemed to come. Frogs! I remembered my first night out with Mother. That night we had feasted on frogs. They were delicious. Here I had my breakfast as well as my water.

I rushed forward and burst forth from the grass. There were many splashes.

31

"Ya dumb kid," said an angry voice. There on a rock by the edge of the pond was a large, angry-looking raccoon.

I stopped short.

"Look what you did," he went on. "I almost had the biggest one of the bunch when you came charging out like you had no sense in your head and scared them all out of their wits."

He sort of hissed in disgust and leaped away from the rock, disappearing in the trees. I never even got a chance to say that I was sorry.

I *was* sorry. I had no idea that my noise could scare away someone's breakfast. How was I to know that frogs didn't like noise? I guess I would have to find food somewhere else. With a big sigh, I moved on.

I was about to give up when I stumbled on an exciting discovery—the leftovers from

a picnic lunch. There were crusts from sandwiches, two apple cores, a banana peel, some crumbs from a tasty cake, and a whole slice of watermelon. It was a feast! By the time I was finished, I was so full I thought I would burst.

Even though I had made the raccoon angry and scared the frogs away, the rest of the day was going quite well. I couldn't wait to see what else I would find in the forest.

CHAPTER
Seven

My bed was no more comfortable on my second night in the log. I twisted and turned, but it seemed that there was always a knot or a twig poking in my side or jabbing at my back. If I were to use the log for many nights, I should do something about making my bed soft. I did eventually get to sleep in spite of it, and the next thing I knew the sun was up and my stomach was telling me that it was time to get moving.

I went back to the pond for water, but I

ignored the frogs. I'd find a meal somewhere else. Besides, I didn't want any more
raccoons to get mad at me.

I had not gone far when I saw a hedgehog. He, too, was busy looking for his breakfast. I was so excited to see him that I had to
keep myself from calling out excitedly. I ran
quickly to greet him.

The hedgehog looked up suddenly, and
his eyes widened. He backed off a few steps,
and at the look on his face, I slowed down.
Suddenly, he ran away!

Even before I could say a "How-do-you-
do," he was gone. I felt like crying as I
watched him go. What was the matter with
everyone? Why wouldn't they talk to me?
Was there something the matter with me?

A soft rain had started to fall. I was wet
and lonesome and miserable. I didn't feel
like breakfast anymore. I decided to head for

the log.

Even though I did not have Mother, my family, or even any friends, the knots and lumps of the log seemed to welcome me. At least here I felt safe and, in a strange way, even at home. Maybe I should just get used to being alone.

CHAPTER
Eight

Since I didn't have anyone to help me, I was going to have to decorate my log home by myself. I thought for a while about what I needed. Then, after measuring the inside of the log, I set off.

There were lots of kinds of grass to choose from. Long grass, short grass, dark green grass, even grass with yellow flowers on top. It was hard to pick just one, so I took some of each. I carried the grass back to my log and laid it across the front.

Now for some moss. I had to walk a bit farther this time, since moss grew in the shady parts of the forest. I walked deeper and deeper into the woods, looking for the

perfect kind of moss that would go on my bed.

Just ahead, behind a big pine tree, there was a large rock that was covered with pretty green moss. It was perfect! I wished I could carry the whole rock back with me, but it was much too heavy. So I pulled off as much as I could carry and started back for my log.

I spent most of the afternoon working on my log. No one offered to help me, even though once in a while I heard different animals moving around in the bushes. I could tell they were watching me. Maybe they were curious about how a skunk fixes up a log home. But no one came out to say hello. No one at all.

I just ignored them and finished up. When the last piece of soft moss was in place, I was tired. It was hard work fixing up my log. But I was real proud of my new home. If only I had a friend who could come over to play . . . then it would be perfect.

CHAPTER
Nine

It was plain to me that no one in the forest wished to make friends with me. Although I couldn't understand it, I guessed I would need to just accept it.

I set out to find some berries, but the picking was slim. I found only a few, and what I did find were small and green. They were not very good eating. Then I remembered the picnic area! Was it possible that more food would be there today? I had better go check it out.

To my delight, I found that there had been another picnic. I also found that there were other animals who had decided to take advantage of the fact. Two raccoons were on a large barrel that seemed to be filled with good things. A possum was enjoying himself in a smaller barrel closer to me. A large bear, followed closely by two young cubs, came around the end of the picnic table.

I didn't intend to cut in on their eating, but I didn't think that they would mind if I just checked out the crumbs here and there. I approached very quietly, not wanting to disturb any of them. I was almost to the small barrel when the bear swung up and her nose began to busily sniff the wind. With one alarmed *woof*, she swung away from the barrel and was gone, her two cubs scurrying along in an effort to keep up with her. I don't know what it was that made her decide to leave. I guess that it was just me again.

In her haste to rush off, the bear had tipped the big barrel over on its side. This

was a big help to me. I
could walk right in
and thoroughly go
over its contents.
My, there were a lot
of good things there.

After eating most of
what I could, I moved on to the other side of
the picnic area. The two possums were argu-
ing over a banana they had found. I couldn't
understand why they should be fighting.
There was plenty for everyone. I moved over
to the second barrel to ask an overweight
raccoon if he'd mind sharing it with me. He
took one look at me, squealed, and left me
the whole thing. The possums dropped the
banana and scampered away just as fast.

I had decided not to let it bother me
and went right to work on the first course.
The food was plentiful and tasty, and I soon

had filled my little tummy again. I might not be any good at making friends, but at least I had enough to eat.

CHAPTER
Ten

The day was bright and sunny. I thought it would be a good day for a walk. Maybe I could explore a new part of the forest.

I headed off in a direction that I had never taken before. The path was well worn, so I felt sure that lots of animals were around. Sure enough, I had not gone far when I met some bush rabbits. They did not stay to talk or play, so I continued down the path. I saw a mother coon who was busy scolding her offspring. I knew they wouldn't be in the mood for a neighborly chat, so I moved around them and hurried on down the path.

After walking a few more minutes, I came upon a meadow. It was lovely! The breeze stirred the flowers, making them wave. Here and there crickets chirped, and small animals ran from tree to tree. All of a sudden, I wished that my log were here in this meadow. It was so pretty and happy.

Just then I turned my head. There, only a few feet away, stood a fawn, who was quietly eating the grass. I held my breath, watching her. She was the prettiest animal I had ever seen. I stood quietly. I did not want her to run away.

Suddenly, she lifted her head and looked right at me. I did not speak or move, though I wanted to with all of my heart. Then the most amazing thing happened. She smiled.

"Hello," she said shyly.

"Hello," I said back in surprise.

"Are you new here?"

I nodded my head.

"Do you live in the meadow?" the fawn asked.

"No, I live that way—in my log house," I told her. I wanted to pinch myself! This was like a dream.

I was just going to ask her where she lived when her mother walked up. She stopped short and looked at me, then at her baby, and then back to me.

"Oh my! Come along, Cassandra," she said to the fawn. "Let's not stay here any longer." And away they went.

I decided to leave then, too. All of the joy had gone out of my day. I headed for my log. It was some distance back, and I knew that by the time I reached it, I would be sleepy and ready for bed.

But as I walked home, I couldn't stop

the tears that ran down my face. I was so
close! So close to making a friend. And then,
just like always, they ran away. I cried even
harder.

C H A P T E R
Eleven

I went back to the meadow each day, hoping that I would find the young deer again. But I did not see the fawn in the meadow that day, nor the next, nor the next. I had almost given up, but I decided to give it one more try. Besides, the meadow was such a nice place to be that I loved my time there, even if it did mean that I spent it all alone.

Suddenly, a loud noise startled me. Without knowing why, I knew that something was wrong—terribly wrong. Then I heard a rushing as frantic feet raced toward me. I ran—as quickly as I could run—down the path to where there was a sharp rise so that I might get a better look to see what was happening.

There was the fawn! She was running wildly. Fast on her flying heels was a full-grown coyote. When it finally got through to me that the coyote was after her, my heart began to pound. The coyote was not going to give up. Even I could see that.

There was another sound, and I whirled around to see the fawn's mother running forward. Her eyes were wide with fear as she looked around. "Oh no . . . oh, someone, please help!"

There wasn't much time. I ran down the slope and looked for anything that could help. But what could I do—especially against a mean animal like a coyote?

All at once, a strange feeling passed through my body. Maybe there was a way—a way that I had not even been aware of. My body was all twitchy inside—like something was trying to get out.

I let the fawn pass by and then whirled sharply, stamped my feet, and threw up my tail. My aim was good. A sharp cry arose from the coyote. He stopped his running and turned back down the path. As he left the meadow, he was still yipping and crying. Occasionally he would stop his running to rub at his eyes with his paws and even roll his head in the grass.

I couldn't believe it! What had I done? The coyote had run away, but I could still hear his distant yipping. The fawn had collapsed in the tall meadow grass, and her mother had moved over to comfort her.

The air was filled with the worst odor I had ever smelled! And it had come from me. Yuck! How awful. What would the deer think of me now?

CHAPTER
Twelve

I didn't want to stick around to explain myself. It was too embarrassing. So I tucked my tail between my legs and started to slink away. Maybe if I was quiet enough, they wouldn't see me leave. And I would never come back to the meadow again.

"How can I ever thank you?" the mother deer said.

I stopped and turned around. My mouth hung open in surprise.

"Are you talking to me?" I asked.

"Oh, if it hadn't been for you, my baby . . ." Her voice was filled with sadness. "Thank you," she said again. "Thank you so much. If ever . . . if ever there is anything . . .

anything that we can do . . ."

I couldn't believe that she was speaking
to me—I mean, with the nasty smell and all.
And here she was, wanting to do something
for me in return. I guess the smell didn't
matter as much to her.

"Well . . . there is one thing," I said,
looking at the ground. I was afraid to ask.

"Yes?" she asked again. "Please . . .
please continue. I know that there isn't
much that I can do. . . ."

I gulped and gathered my courage.

"If . . . if it isn't too much . . . I mean . . .
if you don't mind . . . could . . . could—" I
swallowed hard and then blurted it out.
"Could we be friends?"

After I had said it, I wished that I hadn't
been so bold. What if she turned away or
laughed at me?

But she didn't. Her eyes opened wide in

surprise. "Oh yes . . . yes. For always. Yes! Indeed, you are our friend—our most *special* friend."

Slowly I took in her words, and then a grin spread over my face.

"Jiminy whiz!" I said excitedly.

CHAPTER
Thirteen

Mrs. Deer tapped her daughter and said softly, "Cassandra, we have a new friend. This is . . . I'm sorry, I don't know your name."

"Fuzzle," I said.

"This is Fuzzle," the mother deer continued. The way that she spoke my name made it sound pretty.

Cassandra struggled to her feet and raised her head. She even managed a slight smile. I smiled back.

"Hi, Fuzzle," she said. And then she added quietly, "Thank you."

"Oh, it was nothing," I stammered, embarrassed by the whole thing. "I was so afraid. . . ."

"Where do you live, Fuzzle?" Cassandra asked.

"I live in a hollow log down by the creek bed. Just a little ways down the trail from the pond. The creek is almost dry now over near my log."

"It dries up in the summer heat, but if we get a good rain it will fill again," said Mrs. Deer. "We are very fortunate here in Wonder Meadow that we always have the pond for our water supply."

"Wonder Meadow?" I said. "Is that the name of this beautiful place?"

The deer looked around her with pride in her eyes.

"Yes, this is Wonder Meadow. And it is beautiful, isn't it?"

"I love it," I said frankly. "I wish that my log were over here."

"I don't suppose it could be moved."

"I don't think so. It's pretty big."

"Maybe you could find another log— over here," Mrs. Deer said.

"Oh yes!" I agreed. "I would love that."

Cassandra began to move around. She flexed her leg muscles, as though testing to see if they would still work. I wondered if she would be stiff and sore after her hard run, but she looked as graceful as ever.

"Are you feeling better?" I asked.

"Oh, much better. Thank you, Fuzzle."

"I must let you go," I said to them. "I'm sure that you have things to do before the sun goes down. Will I see you again?" I asked quickly, not wanting them to go away.

"Oh yes. We will watch for you. We feed here in the meadow almost every night." Then with big smiles and good-byes, we parted our ways.

I headed back to my log home, almost silly with happiness. I had a friend—my first *real* friend. I was no longer all alone. I had a friend.

No, that was not right. I had two friends.

CHAPTER
Fourteen

I woke up the next morning and stretched and yawned. The way I rescued Cassandra came back to me, and I smiled. It was so good to know I could go to Wonder Meadow today and talk with friends. I was eager to get going.

But as soon as I left my log, I was surrounded! It looked like all the animals in the forest were gathered around my front door. They were clapping and cheering and trying to shake my hand all at once.

"What's going on?" I asked. "What are you all doing here?"

"We're here to say thank-you!" said an owl.

"THANK YOU, FUZZLE!" everyone shouted together.

"You see, Fuzzle," said the owl. "That old coyote has been an enemy of the forest for some time. None of us could ever get him to leave us alone. And then yesterday, all at once, you really got him! We're so glad you were there to help Cassandra."

Another cheer went up from all the animals.

"Well," I said. "I hardly even know what happened. One minute that mean coyote was chasing Cassandra, and the next he was running away from that terrible smell."

"Don't you see?" asked the owl. "You're a skunk. That's what skunks do best."

"They do?" I asked.

"Yes. And that's why we were never sure if we should get too close to you. We didn't want to get sprayed by you."

"Oh my," I said. "I would never have sprayed you just to be mean."

"We know that now," the owl said. "And we all want to be your friends."

"Jiminy whiz!" I yelled, and everyone laughed.

CHAPTER
Fifteen

I was just getting to know all my new friends when Cassandra and Mrs. Deer approached. They were each smiling and looked like they shared a secret.

"We have good news for you, Fuzzle," said Mrs. Deer.

Cassandra was too excited to keep quiet anymore. "We found a new home for you in Wonder Meadow!" she exclaimed. "It's a log, much like this one, only bigger. It's dry and in a place where it should never be reached by flood waters. It's almost hidden, so it should be private. It is close to the meadow and not far from the pond or the picnic area."

I felt about ready to burst.

"Can we see it?" I asked and almost forgot to be polite. "Could you show us?"

"Of course," she answered and turned to lead the way.

We all followed her. The other animals of the forest seemed just as excited as I was.

When we reached the site, Cassandra had to take us right up to the log, it was so hidden. I don't think that any of us would have spotted it on our own. I wondered how she had ever found it. Inside, it was perfect. Way toward the back was a perfect sleeping room. It was soft with the dust of the rotting log. And with a little moss and some dry leaves, it would be cozy and warm.

I went back out

to tell Cassandra that it was just what I had been looking for. As soon as I came out, my new friends took turns going in to check over the new home. They were as excited as I was. And each of them in turn told me it was quite the nicest skunk home that they had ever been in.

I thanked Cassandra the best that I could. She hung her head shyly, but she gave me a delightful smile. I knew we were going to be the best of friends.

All the other animals began talking at once.

"How can we help?"

"What do you need?"

"How do you want it fixed?"

I laughed at their excitement. "I use moss and leaves," I answered them. Then they all scurried off in many directions. It wasn't long before they were back with mouthfuls of soft, dry moss.

"You go in, we'll bring you the material, and you can arrange it just the way you want it," Cassandra told me.

The leaves and moss came, load after load. I pushed and poked and arranged it— just where I wanted it—and still it kept coming. I poked in some more and tucked a bit more about my feet, and then pushed at the head and padded my bed a bit. It looked so inviting that I could hardly keep myself from crawling into it.

I came out and announced, "All done! And now I'm going to go and test it out."

I curled up as tightly as I could and let my body sink deeply into the softness of my bed. But it wasn't just my new log that made me so happy. It was knowing that I had friends who loved me and wanted to help me. That's what really made Wonder Meadow feel like home.